Blue's Clues

A Picnic with Blue

Published by Advance Publishers, L.C.
www.advance-publishers.com

©2000 Viacom International Inc. All rights reserved. Nickelodeon,
Blue's Clues and all related titles, logos and characters are trademarks of
Viacom International Inc.
Visit Blue's Clues online at www.nickjr.com

Written by Ronald Kidd
Art layout by J.J. Smith-Moore
Art composition by David Maxey
Produced by Bumpy Slide Books

ISBN: 1-57973-078-7

Blue's Clues Discovery Series

Hi, there! Today Blue and I decided it would be fun to go on a picnic. Would you like to come along? Great!

What should we bring to our picnic, Blue?
Oh! We'll play Blue's Clues to figure out what
Blue wants to bring to the picnic. What a great
idea! We'll invite everyone!

Hey, let's go to the backyard and pick a good spot for the picnic. Then we can invite Shovel and Pail!

Do you see a good spot? Good thinking!
It's nice and shady under that tree.
Hey, there's Shovel and Pail!

Would you two like to come to our picnic? Maybe you could bring apples for everyone to eat.

Cool! Well, we should get going and invite everyone else.
So long, Shovel and Pail! See you at the picnic!

Hey, this is exciting! Now Shovel, Pail, and Tickety are all coming! Our picnic is getting bigger all the time!

What's that? Oh, you see a clue! That glass on the table is a clue! Okay, we're trying to figure out what Blue wants to bring to the picnic, and our first clue is a glass.

Hmm. I think we need two more clues. Let's keep looking!

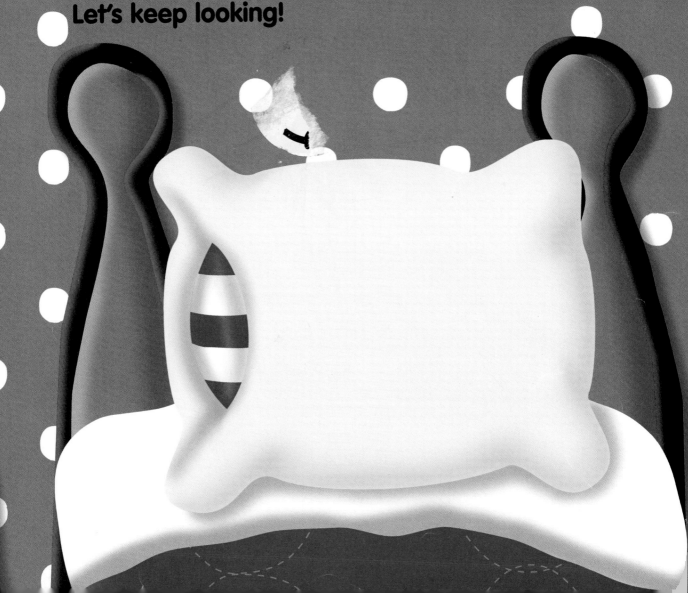

A blanket? Oh! So we'll have something to sit on at the picnic! Sure, we'll be happy to fold it for you. There! You know, it's a lot easier to get something done when you do it with friends.

See you at the picnic, Tickety!

Do you see the jelly? What's that? Oh, there's a clue in the freezer! It's the ice cubes. Now, let's see. Our first clue is a glass, and our second clue is ice cubes. So what could Blue want to bring to the picnic with a glass and ice? I think we need to find our third clue.

You know, working together sure makes sandwich making go fast! Mr. Salt lays out the bread. Mrs. Pepper spreads the peanut butter. And Blue adds the jelly!

But what should I do? Ah. Good idea! I'll find a basket to put all these sandwiches in.

Yummm! Bananas are my favorite. What's that? Another clue? Oh, it's the lemon! Our final clue is a lemon. You know what it's time for? Right! Time to go to our . . . Thinking Chair!

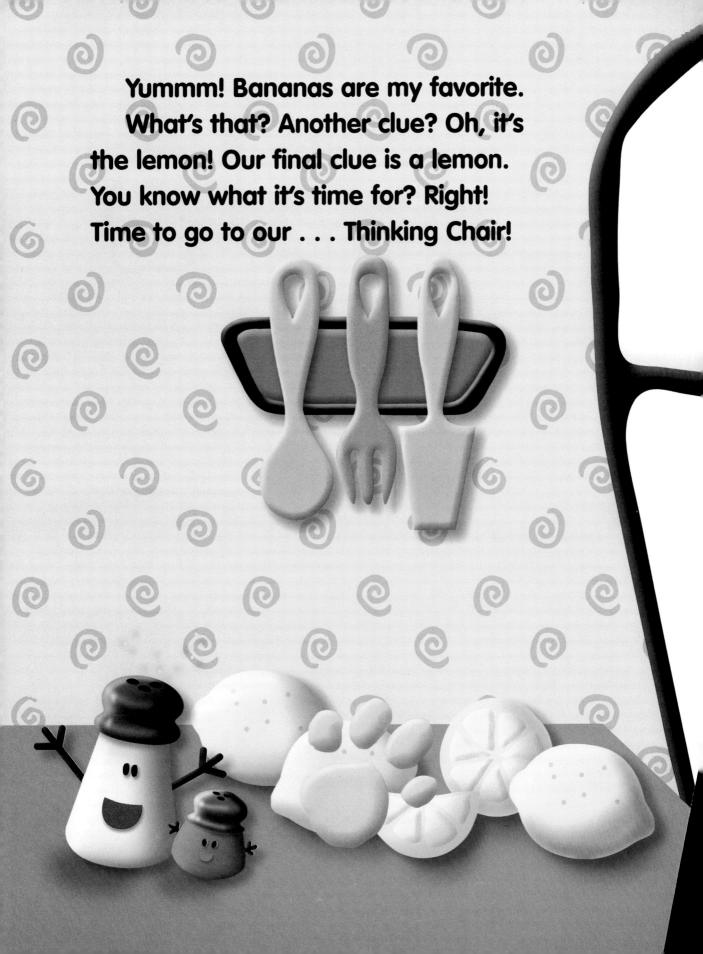

So we're trying to figure out what Blue wants to bring to the picnic with a glass, ice cubes, and a lemon. What do you think she wants to bring?

That's it! Blue wants to bring lemonade. We just figured out Blue's Clues! This lemonade will be perfect for our picnic!

Time for our picnic! There's Tickety's blanket. Shovel and Pail brought their apples. There's the basket of food we helped Mr. Salt and Mrs. Pepper pack. And to top it off, we can have some of Blue's lemonade! It's going to be a great picnic because we all worked together! Thanks for your help today!

BLUE'S "ANTS ON A LOG" SNACK

You will need: celery, peanut butter, and raisins

1. Wash the celery stalks and pat them dry with paper towels.

2. Ask a grown-up to cut the celery into three-inch pieces.

3. Spread peanut butter in the hollow part of the celery.

4. Add the raisins and you've made "ants on a log"!

5. Eat and enjoy!